11
Toilet-bound

Contents

SPOOK 51
PERFECTLY EMPTY IDEALS

YASHIRO HAS LESS THAN A YEAR LEFT.
THAT IS HER PREDETERMINED FUTURE.
BUT HERE, IN THIS FICTIONAL WORLD...
PATCH: SEAL
...SHE CAN GO BEYOND THE LIMITS PLACED ON HER LIFESPAN...
...AND SHE CAN LIVE.

WHAT ...?
IS THAT FOR REAL ...??

GOOD EVENING! I AM NENE YASHIRO, AND I'M ACTUALLY AWAKE.

AH...
THE TRUTH IS... I WOKE UP ON THE WAY BACK FROM THE PARK.

EARRING: TRAFFIC-SAFETY CHARM

BUT HANAKO-KUN BROKE THE CUTE PAINT-BRUSH...

...THAT WAS GOING TO TELL US HOW TO GET HOME...

...AND KNOCKED ME OUT.

HE WAS ACTING KIND OF WEIRD, IS WHAT I'M SAYING.

SO I THOUGHT PRETENDING TO STILL BE UNCONSCIOUS MIGHT HELP M FIGURE OUT WHAT WAS UP WITH HIM.
BUT...

I THINK... I WISH I HADN'T...

SENPAI...

...WOULDN'T HAVE TO DIE...?

?

SHOCK
I'M...
I'M GONNA DIE!??
WAIT...
CAN SOMEONE EXPLAIN THIS...?
DON'T JUST KEEP TALKING LIKE EVERYBODY KNOWS...!

SOON, THIS WORLD WILL BE COMPLETE. UNTIL THEN...
...I'M GOING TO HAVE TO LOCK HER UP.

WHAT...?

—
—
HE'S... GOING TO LOCK ME UP? WHERE!?

WHAT SHOULD I DO...? MAYBE IT'S TIME FOR ME TO WAKE UP...

SEE YA.
YASHIRO IS COMING WITH ME.

PLEASE... AT LEAST TELL THEM WHERE YOU'RE PLANNING TO TAKE ME...

STUPID HANAKO-KUUUN!!!

FLUFF
ふわっ

I WONDER WHERE HE BROUGHT ME...

PEEK
チラ

ボロッ
GRUBBY
...

IT'S...
...A PRISON CELL...

ガチャン
CLANK

W-WAIT!

HANAKO-KUN!

YASHIRO...
YOU'RE AWAKE.
HANA-KO-KUN...
I KNEW IT WAS REALLY YOU.
ガシャ
CLANG

WHAT'S GOING ON?
WHY ARE YOU DOING THIS!?

YOU...

YOU PRETENDED YOU WERE STILL ALIVE...

...AND NOW YOU'RE LOCKING ME UP IN HERE...
WHY...?

WELL...

BEAM
はっ

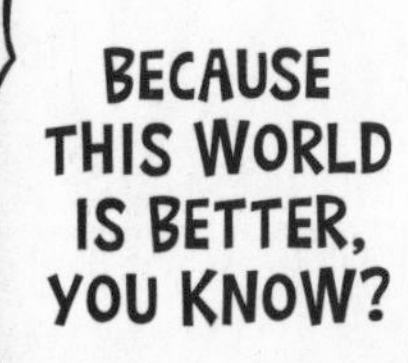
BECAUSE THIS WORLD IS BETTER, YOU KNOW?

I ALWAYS WANTED TO SEE WHAT IT WAS LIKE!
GOING TO SCHOOL WITH YOU, I MEAN.
IT'S ACTUALLY NOT THAT BAD, DON'T YOU THINK?
I-I'M...

...NOT REALLY GOING TO DIE, AM I...?
RIGHT, HANAKO-KUN...?

...
WHY WOULD YOU ASK THAT...?

BECAUSE I...
...HEARD WHAT YOU SAID TO KOU-KUN.

ABOUT ME...
...HAVING LESS THAN A YEAR TO LIVE.

IT'S NOT TRUE, IS IT, HANAKO-KUN?
I...!!

OH...

SO YOU HEARD THAT...
...YASHIRO.
封

...

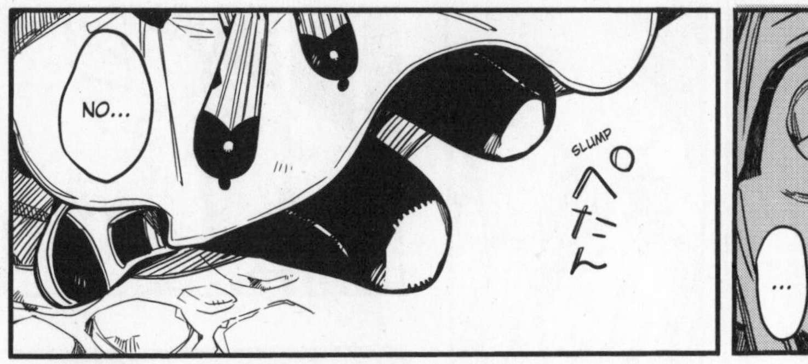
SLUMP
ぺたん
NO...

I'M GOING TO DIE? YOU CAN'T JUST SPRING THAT ON ME OUT OF NOWHERE...
AND WHY...?
WHY DO YOU GET TO DECIDE ALL THIS FOR ME WITHOUT ASKING...?

DRIP
ポタ
DRIP
ポタ

I NEVER HAVE ANY IDEA WHAT YOU'RE THINKING, HANAKO-KUN...

"WHY" ...?

ビク
FLINCH
す
SHFF

GOOD QUESTION. WHY AM I DOING

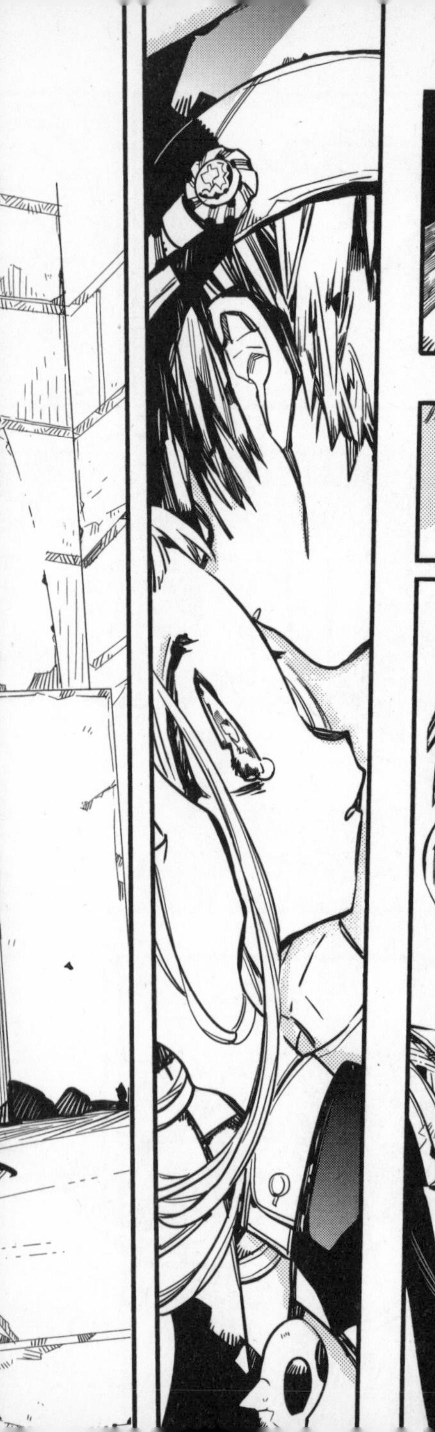

IT'S OKAY.
I'M GOING TO SAVE YOU, YASHIRO.

SO YOU JUST...
...STAY HERE, FOREVER, AND DON'T WORRY ABOUT A THING.
封

HUH?

HANAKO-KUN...WHAT DO YOU MEAN BY "FOREVER" ...?
I'LL BE GOING NOW.
I'LL COME GET YOU WHEN THIS WORLD IS COMPLETE.

WAIT!! HANAKO-K—
ギィィィ
CREEEAK

バタン…
SLAM

SLUMP
ずる…
W...

WAAAH...
NGH...

HONORABLE No. 7.

FLAG: GUIDE
No. 4.
UGH.
WOULD YOU PLEASE NOT USE MY ART MUSEUM WITHOUT MY PERMISSION?

THOUGH I DO APPRECIATE THAT YOU'RE WILLING TO LET ME FINISH MY WORLD.

OH, AND, HONORABLE No. 7...
...DO YOU HAVE ANY INTEREST IN STAYING HERE FOREVER?

......
OF COURSE NOT.
I'LL LEAVE WHEN THE WORLD IS DONE.

YOUR POWER JUST HAPPENS TO BE EXACTLY WHAT I NEED TO KEEP YASHIRO SAFE.
I'M ONLY MAKING USE OF IT FOR HER.

ANYWAY, HURRY UP AND FINISH IT FOR ME, WON'T YOU?
I NEED YOUR PICTURE-PERFECT WORLD FULLY COMPLETED.

GRIN
YES, SIIIR!
I HEAR YOU LOUD AND CLEAR!

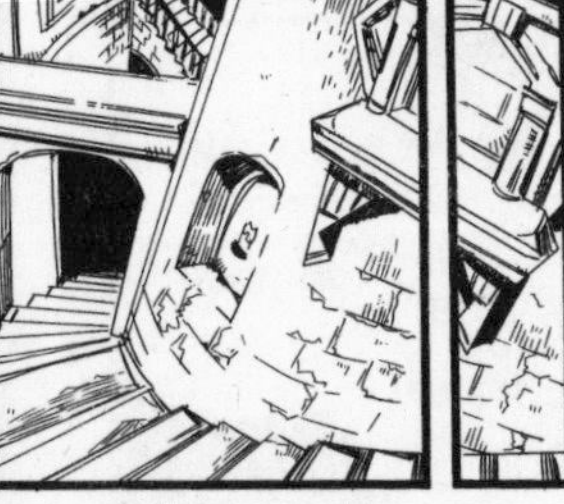

HOW ARE YOU FEELING?
HELLO?

OH!

ARE YOU ALL RIGHT?
HNGH.
NGH...

I THOUGHT I SHOULD COME CHECK ON YOU.
WHAT'S THE MATTER?
WAS HONORABLE No. 7 PICKING ON YOU?
HE...
HE SAID...

OOOH!
HE SAID I'M GOING TO DIE SOON...
PAT
ぽん

YES, I HEARD ABOUT THAT.
BUT YOU DON'T HAVE TO TAKE IT AS SUCH A TRAGEDY.
す
SFF

PEOPLE WHO ARE NEARING DEATH ARE SPECIAL IN ALL KINDS OF WAYS.
THEY CAN SEE SUPER-NATURALS...
...MAKE CONTRACTS WITH THE SEVEN SCHOOL MYSTERIES...
サラ SKRITCH
サラ SKRITCH
DEPENDING ON HOW YOU LOOK AT IT, IT'S NOT THE WORST TRADE.

CHOCOLATE
ALMOND

ぽん
POP

DO YOU LIKE SWEETS?

THESE SHOULD HELP YOU FEEL BETTER.

HANAKO-KUN SAID...
CRUNCH
カリ

...THAT IF I LEAVE HERE, I'LL DIE.
THAT'S WHY HE'S GOING TO TRAP ME IN THIS WORLD.
OR SO I'VE HEARD.

MY PICTURE-PERFECT WORLD HAS ONLY BEEN ABLE TO EXIST THIS LONG...
...BECAUSE OF YOU.

...WHAT DO YOU MEAN?
DON'T YOU KNOW?

A WORLD LIKE THIS, FILLED WITH NOTHING BUT PLEASANT FICTIONS...
...IS WHAT HONORABLE No. 7 HATES MORE THAN ANYTHING.
NORMALLY, HE WOULD WANT TO DESTROY IT AS SOON AS HE FOUND OUT ABOUT IT.

BUT THIS TIME, HE REALIZED.
HE KNEW THAT IN THIS WORLD, YOU COULD *LIVE*.
SO HE COULDN'T DESTROY IT.

HE SAID HE'S GOING TO WAIT UNTIL IT'S FINISHED...
WHAT!?
...AND THEN GO BACK TO THE REAL WORLD ON HIS OWN.

WHAT HONORABLE No. 7 WANTS...

...IS FOR YOU TO LIVE ETERNALLY IN A HAPPY DREAM...
...WITHOUT EVER HAVING TO WORRY ABOUT YOUR IMMINENT DEATH.

HE MUST HAVE REALLY TAKEN A LIKING TO YOU.

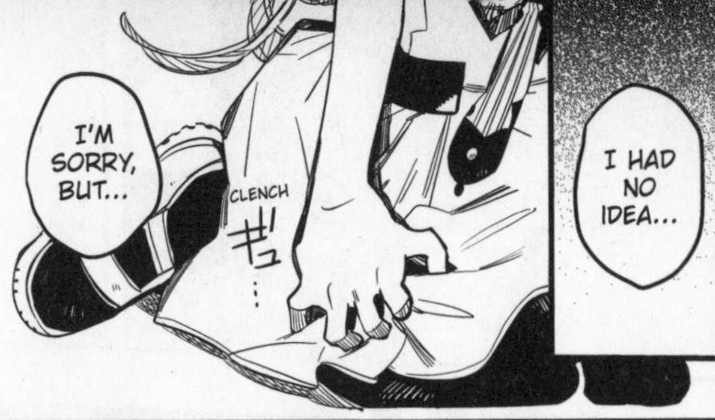

I HAD NO IDEA...
I'M SORRY, BUT...
CLENCH

...THINKING ABOUT ALL OF THESE THINGS MAKES ME SO SAD...

SHIJIMA-SAN.
WOULD YOU MIND HOLDING MY HAND? JUST FOR A MINUTE...
HUH?

ME? REALLY?

MM-HMM.

I WANT SOMEONE TO COMFORT ME...ANYONE OTHER THAN HANAKO-KUN, AT LEAST.

WELL... I GUESS I DON'T REALLY MIND...
SHFF

ぎゅっ
CLENCH
HUH?
すぅ〜〜…
SWOOO
DON'T MOVE!
YANK
!!

HEH!
HEH
HEH
HEH
DON'T TRY ANYTHING FUNNY, OR ELSE...
...YOU'LL GET THE BUSINESS END OF THIS PALETTE KNIFE!!
HUUUH!?
WEREN'T YOU BROKEN DOWN IN TEARS A MINUTE AGO?

THOSE WERE FAKE TEARS!
WHAA-AAAT!?
I REALLY DID HAVE A LOT ON MY MIND...

...BUT WHILE I WAS THINKING...
...I FOUND ALL KINDS OF TOOLS LYING AROUND THE CELL.
TUMBLE
SINCE THEY WERE ALL ART SUPPLIES...

...SEEING THEM KIND OF...
...MADE ME WANT TO DRAW...
AND AS I WAS DRAWING THE REAL WORLD...
...I REALLY DID START TO MISS IT... I WANTED TO GO BACK...

AND THEN I STARTED GETTING ANGRY ...!!!
HUH?

WHAT IS WRONG WITH HIM!? HOW CAN HE DO THIS WITHOUT EVEN TALKING TO ME ABOUT IT!?
HE THINKS HE'S THAT IMPORTANT JUST 'COS HE'S DEAD!?
HE'S ALWAYS KEEPING SECRETS FROM ME!
AND I GET THAT THERE ARE SOME THINGS HE JUST DOESN'T WANT TO TALK ABOUT!
BUT HIM BEING DEAD AND ME BEING ALIVE IS NO REASON TO ACT LIKE THAT!!

I HAVE HAD IT!
THERE'S NO WAY I'M GONNA LET HIM GET HIS WAY...

I WANT TO GO BACK HOME TO THE REAL WORLD!!
AND YOU'RE GOING TO HELP ME...
...SHIJIMA-SAN!

SPOOK 52
PICTURE OF A WISH

AND YOU'RE GOING TO HELP ME...
...SHIJIMA-SAN!

...
YOU REALLY STARTLED ME.

BUT PLEASE DON'T TELL ME...
SHRR
する...

WHACK
AH!
...YOU ACTUALLY THINK YOU CAN THREATEN ME WITH A PALETTE KNIFE...
YOU CAN'T KILL SOME-ONE WITH THIS!
URK!

D-DO WHAT I SAY, OR...
...I'LL POKE YOU! I'LL POKE A HOLE IN YOU!!
SWISH
SWISH
SWISH
SWISH
SWISH
WHAAAA ...?
GRAB
BUT...
...LET ME ASK YOU.

ARE YOU SURE YOU WANT TO LEAVE THIS WORLD?
IF YOU GO BACK TO YOUR OWN...
...YOUR LIFE WILL RUN OUT AND YOU'LL DIE VERY SOON, REMEMBER?
N—
NOT NECES-SARILY!
WE DON'T REALLY KNOW IF THAT'S TRUE!
EVEN IF HE SAYS I'M GONNA DIE...
...IT'S ALL SO SUDDEN, IT DOESN'T FEEL REAL...

WHAT IF IT IS TRUE?

WHAT IF YOUR DEATH...
...REALLY IS JUST AROUND THE CORNER...
...AND THERE'S ABSOLUTELY NO WAY FOR YOU TO AVOID IT?

WHAT THEN?
WOULD YOU STILL GO BACK?

......
OH... ARE YOU OKAY?

YOU'RE SHAKING.
YOU ARE SCARED, AREN'T YOU?

E—

EVEN SO...

...IT SHOULD BE FINE TO LEAVE THIS WORLD!
...I'M SURE... EVERYTHING WILL BE JUST FINE...!

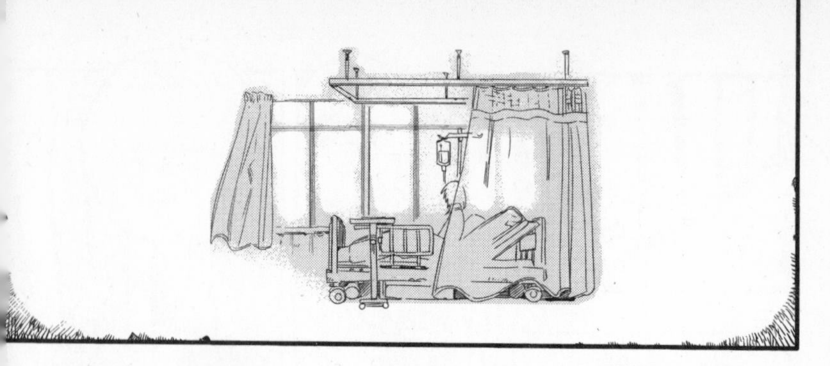

BECAUSE I—
"I'M STILL ALIVE." ...IS THAT WHAT YOU WERE GOING TO SAY?

HUH...?
YOUR HOPE IS BASELESS...
YOU SAY YOU'LL BE FINE, BUT THAT'S JUST WISHFUL THINKING.
IT'S NO BETTER THAN FICTION.

IT'S JUST STUPID.

I KNEW SOMEONE... WHO USED TO TALK LIKE THAT.
BUT NO AMOUNT OF DREAMING EVER CHANGED REALITY.

......
SOMEONE WHO USED TO TALK LIKE ME ...?

WAS IT, BY ANY CHANCE...
...YOUR SPECIAL SOME-ONE?

SPECIAL ...?
YES... IN A SENSE.
BUT IT DOESN'T MATTER.
I'LL NEVER SEE THAT PERSON AGAIN.

WANT ME TO CHANGE THAT?

!!
SHOCK
ビク

TSU...

TSUKASA-KUN...!?
GRIIIN

HOW DID YOU GET HERE...?

YOU CALLED ME, No. 4.
YOU MADE A WISH, DIDN'T YOU? TO "SEE YOUR SPECIAL SOMEONE?"

FLICKER

I ALWAYS COME WHEN SOMEONE MAKES A WISH FROM THE HEART.

SLASH
!!

WHA...
カラ
CLATTER
カラ
CLATTER
ガラ
CLATTER
AND NOW THAT YOU'VE CALLED ME HERE, I'VE GOTTA GRANT YOUR WISH.
WHAT ARE YOU DOING!?
YOU CAN'T JUST...
HONOR-ABLE No. 7 WILL BE MAD AT YOU!
くるっ
WHIRL
HEY.
ビク
JOLT

YOU'RE THE ONE WHO MADE THIS HAPPEN, AREN'T YOU?

THEN YOU'LL HELP, RIGHT?
SINCE YOU'RE THE ONE WHO GOT No. 4 TO FESS UP ABOUT HER WISH.
ME ...?

ALL RIGHT.

READY TO PAY THE PRICE?
SHFF
ス...
THEN LET'S GO, No. 4.

IT'S TIME TO GRANT YOUR WISH.
WHAT...?

ヒュオッ
WHOOSH
WAIT A MINUTE... I DIDN'T AGREE TO THIS!
ふわっ
FLOAT
ACK!
WHAT THE...?
わた
FLAIL
HUH? ME TOO!? WHY!?
わた
FLAIL

PUT ME DOWN, TSUKASA-KUN!
HAVE FUN!
I'M NOT A PART OF THIS!

CLAP
パチン!
TSU-KASA-K—
SHLOOP
ヒュルン!

...IF SENPAI...
...STAYS HERE, SHE WON'T HAVE TO DIE.
SERI-OUSLY?

DAMMIT, HANAKO...SO THAT'S WHAT YOU WERE PLOTTING.
......

YOU KNOW... MAYBE HE'S RIGHT, BUT...
...STAYING HERE FOREVER ...?
THAT'S JUST...

IT'S JUST NOT RIGHT...

......
I...

...I'M STILL HURTING FROM WHEN HONORABLE No. 7 BLASTED ME BACK THERE.
I THOUGHT I WAS GONNA DIE, YOU KNOW.
ドッ
FWOOOM
ゴォ
BACK THERE

I WOULD REALLY APPRECIATE A LITTLE MORE KINDNESS AND CONSIDERATION!
GAAAH! OKAY, I'M SORRY!
THAT MUST HAVE HURT!! THANKS FOR SHIELDING ME!
交通
TCH.
THOUGHT-LESS EARRING BOY.
JUST CAN'T PLEASE SOME PEOPLE...
HAAH...

I KNOW YOU HAVE A LOT TO THINK ABOUT...
...WITH RADISH-SENPAI AND HON-ORABLE No. 7.
BUT PULL YOURSELF TOGETHER!
WHAP
YEOWCH!!
WHAT WAS THAT FOR!!?
JOLT
I WISH YOU'D STOP BEING SO WISHY-WASHY, MINAMOTO-KUN.
AFTER THAT HIGH-AND-MIGHTY SPEECH YOU GAVE ME...

...YOU'D BETTER TAKE RESPONSI-BILITY AND DO WHAT YOU SAID YOU WOULD!

FWIP

...

...YEAH.
YOU'RE RIGHT.

OKAY!
ギュ...
CLENCH

OKAY... I'M GONNA GO KICK No. 4'S BUTT!!
DUDUN

RAR
NO, YOU'RE NOT!!
HUH!?

WHY NOT?
FORGET HANAKO—WE CAN PUT A STOP TO ALL THIS IF WE JUST BEAT No. 4, RIGHT?
ARE YOU STUPID, MINAMOTO-KUN?
I MEAN, YOU'RE RIGHT, BUT IF IT WAS THAT EASY TO BEAT HER, WE WOULDN'T BE IN THIS MESS!

AND YOU KNOW HONORABLE No. 7 WILL TRY TO STOP YOU...
...SO YOU CAN RUSH IN ALL YOU WANT, STUPID EARRING BOY, BUT YOU'LL JUST GET YOURSELF...

スコーン
KER-THWACK
...KILLED !??
!?
ビクッ
FLINCH

WHAT THE—WHAT HAPPENED!?
ばっ
WHOOSH
BULLIES!? IS SOMEONE BULLYING ME!?

ヨロ…
HOBBLE

A PAINTBRUSH ...?
TOTTER
TOTTER

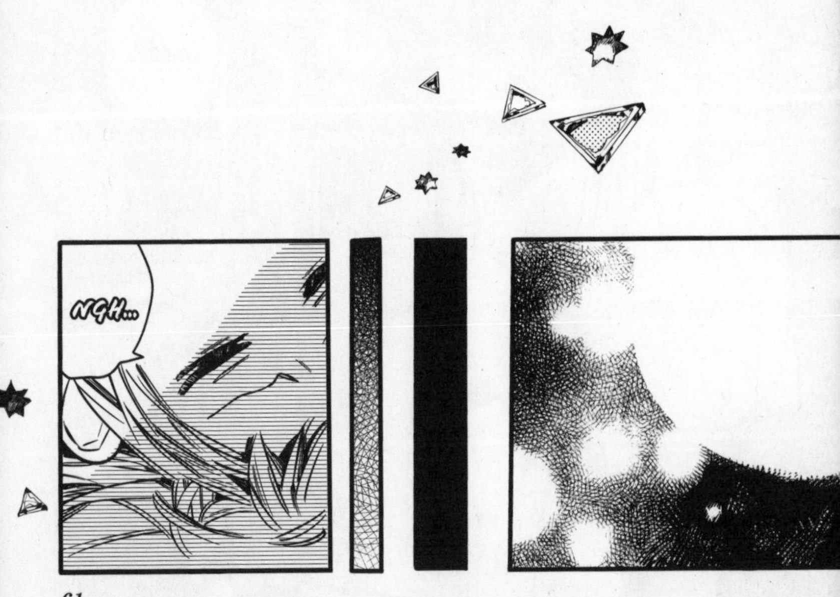
NGH...

ぱちっ
BLINK

ガばっ
JOLT

RETURNING PATIENTS
EXAMINATION ROOM
IN LINE
WHERE...
...AM I?

No. RECEPTION
......
GULP
PEDIATRICS

IT LOOKS LIKE...A HOSPITAL... BUT WHY...?
IS...IS ANYBODY HERE?

OPERATION IN PROGRESS

OUTPATIENTS
THERE'S NOBODY HERE...?

ヒソ
PSST
THAT'S WHAT I HEARD TOO.
ヒソ
PSST
...SO THEY SAY.
ヒソ
PSST

WHOOSH
ばっ
WHO'S THERE!?

THE POOR THING.
SO YOUNG TOO...

NOOOO!
ISN'T ANYBODY HERE!?
SHIJIMA-SAN! I'LL EVEN TAKE TSUKASA-KUN!
WAAAAH!
ダダダダダ
STOMP STOMP STOMP STOMP STOMP

SHIJIMA-SAN!
440
WEST WING

WHAT... WHAT A RELIEF...
HFF... WHEW...
UM, WHERE IN THE WORLD ...?
......

SHIJIMA-
SAN...?
HFF...
HFF...

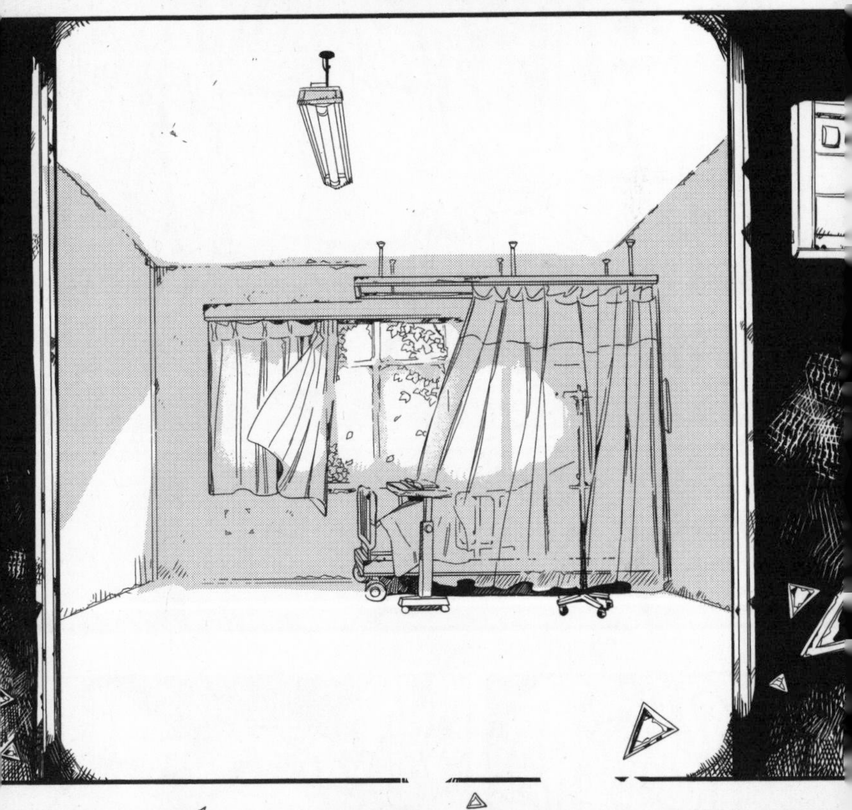

WH—

WHO'S THAT...?

SPOOK 53
IMPERFECT SECRECY

HAVE YOU HEARD THE RUMOR?
THE ONE ABOUT "SHIJIMA-SAN OF THE ART ROOM"?
SHE WAS REALLY GOOD AT DRAWING PICTURES.
BUT HER FAMILY DIDN'T WANT HER TO GO INTO THE ARTS...
...SO RATHER THAN STOP DRAWING FOREVER...
Kamome Academy
STUDENT IDENTIFICATION CAR
This card certifies that the student pictured i
YEAR: 3
CLA
NAME: MEI SH
BIRTHDATE: 19
ADDRESS:
ISSUED AT:
SCHOOL NAME
PRINCIPAL:
STAMP: KAMOME ACADEMY

...SHE KILLED HERSELF.
AND NOW...
...HER SPIRIT STILL HAUNTS THE ART ROOM.
IT REALLY IS...
...JUST SO STUPID.

すう

FICTION IS SO WORTH-LESS.

SHIJIMA-SAN? WHAT ARE YOU DOING...?

WHAT AM I DOING?
I'M MAKING MY WISH COME TRUE, THAT'S ALL.

CLACK
CLACK
CLACK
I ONLY HAVE ONE WISH.

AND IT'S TO KILL...
...MEI SHIJIMA.
WHA—
N—
STOMP
STOMP
STOMP
STOMP

NOOOOO!!!
URK!
WHAAAAAM
KAPOW
CRASH
TWITCH
EXCUSE ME...WOULD YOU PLEASE STAY OUT OF MY WAY?
THIS IS NONE OF YOUR BUSI—
STRAIN
STRAIN
STRAIN
STRAIN
STRAIN
KILLING IS WRONG! KILLING IS WRONG!!
SHFF
す...

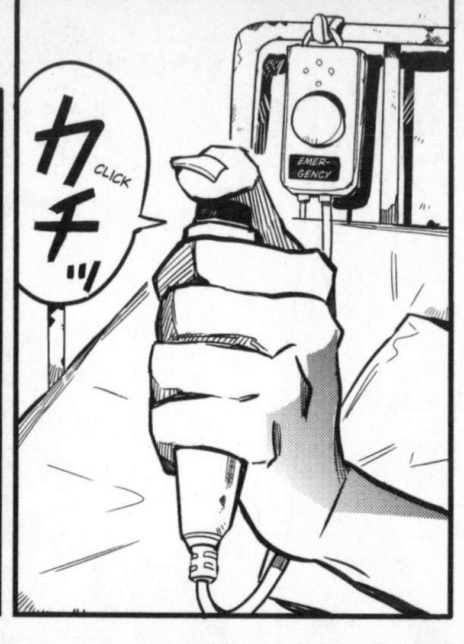
カチッ
CLICK
EMER-
GENCY

ズ…
LOOM

ズズ…
LOOM

ぞろ…
SWARM
YOU CALLED?
WHAT'S THE MATTER?
HOW ARE YOU FEELING?
WHA...?

YOU'LL BE BETTER IN NO TIME.
WH-WHAT!?
WHAT'S HAPPEN-ING!?

...ANNOYING PESTS.

CHAK
チャ

ぐわ
SLIP

ぱしっ
GRAB
!
ヒソ…
PSST
This way.
パラ
PATTER
パラ
PATTER
OH, WHAT A SHAME...
SHE GOT AWAY.

タ TEP
タ TEP
タ TEP
たっ TEP
HFF... HFF...
たったっ TEP TEP
ぎゅん YANK
WOW... THAT WAS ENOUGH TO GIVE A GIRL A HEART ATTACK.
LIKE, A SUSPICIOUS PERSON RANDOMLY SHOWS UP IN YOUR HOSPITAL ROOM WITH A KNIFE?
I JUST HIT THE NURSE CALL BUTTON WITHOUT EVEN THINKING ABOUT IT...
コソ... SNEAK
ARE YOU ALL RIGHT?
HFF HFF
MM-HMM...
I'M FINE... BUT...

...WHAT ARE YOU DOING?
ZH
30...
35 CM...
ZH
ZH
ZH
IS THIS REALLY AN ANKLE...!?
IT'S SO FAT... WAIT, ARE YOU...
... DESCENDED FROM ELEPHANTS !!?
BRUUUUUMP
パオーン
WHY WOULD YOU SAY THAT?

LET ME GET A CLOSER LOOK!
WHAT IS WRONG WITH THIS GIRL!!?
NOOOOO!

...WAIT.
PAUSE
はた

I FEEL LIKE...
...THIS HAS HAPPENED BEFORE.

COME TO THINK OF IT, NOW THAT I REALLY LOOK AT HER...
...SHE KINDA LOOKS LIKE SHIJIMA-SAN...?
STARE
じろ
STARE
じろ

WAIT, HOLD ON...

THEIR FACES ARE EXACTLY THE SAME!

ARE YOU...

...THE LIVING SHIJIMA-SAN?
......
...YES.

SHI JI MA
THAT'S ME.
I'M SHIJIMA-SAN!
SMILE
!!

FLASHBACK
...MEI SHIJIMA.
WHICH MEANS SHIJIMA-SAN'S WISH IS TO KILL HERSELF FROM WHEN SHE WAS ALIVE.
AH!
AND THAT MEANS... IT MEANS...

WHAT DOES IT MEAN...?
HMMMM...
...

BY THE WAY, WHAT BRINGS YOU HERE?
WELL... ACTUALLY, I DON'T EVEN KNOW WHERE THIS IS...AND I HAVE TO GET BACK HOME SOON...
SO YOU'RE LOST?
WOULD YOU LIKE ME TO SHOW YOU TO THE EXIT?
WHAT!?
RADIOLOGY

SHIJIMA-SAN YOU KNOW WHERE WE ARE!?
BEEEEAM
YOU'LL HELP ME!?

I WILL!
BUT...

SQUEEZE

...ONLY IF...
...YOU DO ME A FAVOR FIRST.

STEAM
ホカ
STEAM
ホカ

EEEEEEE!
WOOOOW! IT LOOKS SO GOOD!

ADMISSIONS DESK
RADIOLOGY
AREN'T PANCAKES THE BEST!?
YOURS LOOK GOOD TOO, NENE-CHAN!
UM... SHIJIMA-SAN.

CALL ME MEI-CHAN.
PLEASE? ♥
MEI-CHAN.
SNAP
MENU
FOOD
PANCAKES

THIS IS THE FAVOR YOU WANTED?
YES! ♥
AFTER-HOURS ADMISSIONS
MENU
DRINK
COFFEE
MILK TEA
FOOD
PANCAKES

NOM
YUMMY! DO YOU
ANT SOME,
ENE-CHAN?

SAY AHHHH! ♥
HERE!
HRM...
NOPE.

THIS IS NO TIME...
...TO SIT BACK AND EAT SNACKS.

SO YOU HEARD THAT...
...YASHIRO.

NENE-CHAN.

YOU DON'T WANT IT TO GET COLD... DO YOU?

HERE.
JUST A BITE.

ぱく
NOM

MUNCH
もぐ…
MUNCH
もぐ… もぐ
MUNCH

ごくん
GULP

WHEW
ほ
......
THAT'S GOOD.

NOM
ぱく
NOM
ぱく
NOM
ぱく...
HEE-HEE.

THE CALORIES FROM THAT PANCAKE WENT STRAIGHT TO YOUR ANKLES.
ガーン
CLAAAANG
WH-WH-WH-WHY DO YOU KEEP BULLYING ME ABOUT THAT!?

ZOOM
ズン!
DO YOU WANT TO ORDER ANOTHER?
YEAH!
MENU
THAT'S JUST TOO BIG!
WE'LL GET SO FAT!
PSST... PSST.
PSST... PSST.

THE POOR THING.
THE POOR THING...
OPERATING ROOM
TREATMENT ROOM

カ
ラッ
EMPTY
AHHH, THAT WAS DELICIOUS!

IT'S BEEN SO LONG...
...SINCE I'VE GOTTEN TO EAT PANCAKES WITH A FRIEND.

THANK YOU FOR HANGING OUT WITH ME.
I HAD A LOT OF FUN!
ME TOO...
GRIN
GRIN
GRIN

AH!
I COULDN'T HELP IT... I JUST SAT HERE AND HAD FUN.
WHY AM I LIKE THIS...?
TEA PARTY

UMMM...
YOU DO REALLY KNOW HOW TO GET OUT OF HERE, RIGHT?
YES, OF COURSE I DO.

I SHOULD BE...
...GETTING BACK SOON MYSELF.

GET-TING BACK?

...THERE'S THIS PICTURE.

I'M IN THE MIDDLE OF DRAWING IT.
IT'S AN AS-SIGNMENT...
...FOR THE ART PROGRAM I'M IN.

AN ART PROGRAM...?
YUP! FOR PEOPLE GOING ON TO ART SCHOOL.
YOU GET TO CHOOSE A PROGRAM WHEN YOU BECOME A SECOND-YEAR, 'MEMBER?
SCIENCE, LITERATURE, ART, OR P.E.

SO YOU PLAN TO GO TO ART SCHOOL, MEI-CHAN?
YEAH!
MY PARENTS ARE SUP-PORTING ME TOO.

SO I HAVE TO GIVE IT MY ALL!
CLENCH
ムン
COOL.

HUH...?

IN THE RUMORS...
...SHIJIMA-SAN'S FAMILY WAS AGAINST HER GOING INTO ART.
THAT'S WHY SHE KILLED HERSELF...AT LEAST, THAT'S WHAT I HEARD.

...WAS THAT NOT THE TRUTH?

I HAVE TO TAKE THE PRAC-TICAL EXAM...
...BUT I HAVE NO TIME.
I MEAN, I DON'T LIKE THE IDEA THAT MEI-CHAN...
...WOULD KILL HERSELF.

BUT...
PSST...
PSST PSST.
...PSST... PSST PSST...

SHIVER
PSST PSST... PSST. PSST
PSST PSST PSST. PSST
PSST PSST PSST... PSST
PSST PSST... PSST. PSST
SHOCK
HUH!?
WHAT'S HAPPEN-ING!?
MEI-CHAN...
NENE-CHAN.
PSST PSST PSST... PSST
CLATTER

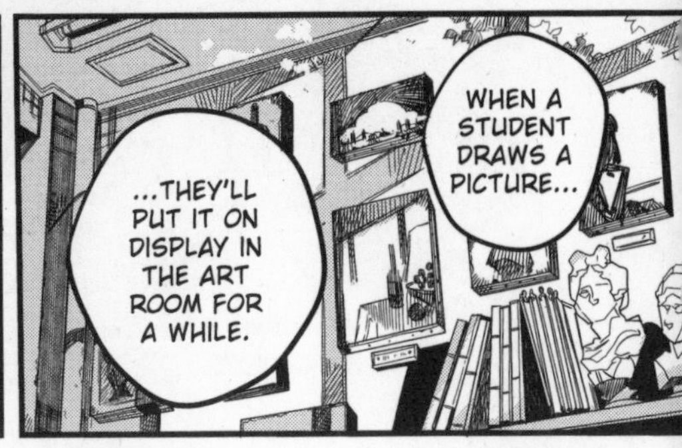
WHEN A STUDENT DRAWS A PICTURE...
...THEY'LL PUT IT ON DISPLAY IN THE ART ROOM FOR A WHILE.

SO WHEN I...
...FINISH MINE...

...WILL YOU COME SEE IT?

SHE'S A LOST CAUSE.
THERE'S NO HOPE.
POOR THING.

SHE'S DRAWING AGAIN.
BUT...
PSST
...IT'S A VERY SERIOUS DISEASE.
LATELY, SHE'S BEEN SLEEPING ALL THE TIME.
SHE DOESN'T EAT MUCH EITHER.
PSST
PSST

IT WON'T BE LONG NOW—

SHE'S GOING TO DIE SOON.

MEI-CHAN...
HAAH...
SERIOUSLY... IT'S SO STUPID.

RUMORS ARE WORTHLESS— NO BETTER THAN FICTION.
ギュ
CLENCH
I...
...AM NOT GOING TO DIE.

POOR THING.
THE POOR THING.
IT WON'T BE LONG NOW.
SHE'S GOING TO DIE SOON.
MEI-CHAN...
HAAH ...
SERIOUSLY... IT'S SO STUPID.
RUMORS ARE WORTHLESS.
I...
...AM NOT GOING TO DIE.

COLOR
COLOR
COLOR

SPOOK 54
SELF-PORTRAIT

I DON'T KNOW...
...WHO IT WAS THAT STARTED THE RUMOR ANYMORE.
MEI SHIJIMA
I DON'T REMEMBER.

HEY, DID YOU KNOW?

I HEARD THE GIRL WHO DREW THIS...
...DIED BEFORE SHE GRADUATED.
NO WAY!
THE POOR THING.
I HAD NO IDEA.
WAIT.
HOW DID SHE DIE?
...
I DON'T KNOW.
WAS SHE SICK?
MAYBE IT WAS AN ACCI-DENT.
OR A MURDER!
OR MAYBE...
...IT WAS SUICIDE.

ヒソ
PSST
WHOA, THAT MAKES SENSE!
LIKE HER PARENTS DIDN'T WANT HER TO GO INTO ART OR SOMETHING?
WHAT? SO SHE KILLED HERSELF?
ヒソ
PSST
A LOT OF ARTISTS ARE MENTALLY ILL.
THE PICTURE IS KINDA SCARY TOO...
PSST
I DON'T LIKE IT...
ヒソ
PSST
ヒソ
PSST
HEY, I HEARD THERE'S A GHOST IN THE ART ROOM.
DO YOU THINK IT'S THE GIRL WHO DREW THAT...?
WHAT IF IT HAS ALL OF HER EVIL RESENTMENT INSIDE IT?
THAT'S SCARY!
I WAS JUST A MODEST LIT-TLE GHOST...
...BUT THE NEXT THING I KNEW...
...I HAD A SEAT AMONG THE SEVEN SCHOOL MYSTERIES.
FOUR

I AM A SUPER-NATURAL WHO PAINTS A FICTIONAL WORLD INSIDE A DRAWING.
BRUSH BRUSH BRUSH
BRUSH BRUSH
ONE WHO LOCKS THE LIVING AWAY INSIDE THAT WORLD.

"SHIJIMA-
SAN OF THE
ART ROOM."
ペタ…
BRUSH
....

I HATE ART.
THEN WHY DON'T YOU JUST STOP!?
にゅっ
NYOOP

ROLL ゴロ
ROLL ゴロ

TOSS ポイッ
PLEASE GO AWAY.
WAAH!

NO GOOD EVER COMES FROM DEALING WITH YOU.
WHAT ARE YOU DOING HERE?
I HEARD ABOUT No. 3.

DID YOU COME TO TAKE MY HEART TOO?

STAAARE じー
C'MON!

I'M NOT GONNA DO THAT.
I'M HERE TODAY...
...TO ASK YOU TO DO ME A FAVOR.
SKFF スタ
SKFF スタ
SKFF スタ

TMP
タ—ンッ

DRAW ME A PICTURE...
...No. 4.
YOU CAN'T STOP DRAWING ANYWAY, RIGHT?
封

TMP
カタン
SKRIT
サラサラ
SKRIT
ポンッ
POOF
YIPES!
OH?
A CLONE OF ME.
プイ
TURN
WE SHARE A CONSCIOUS-NESS, SO YOU CAN GO AHEAD AND TALK TO HER.
TALKING TO YOU DIRECTLY IS EXHAUSTING.
ガーン
CLAAAANG
COOL! GOT IT!
N-N-N-N-NOOOOO!

I DON'T WANT TO TALK TO HIM EITHEEEER!
AAAAHH!
HAAH...

I HATE DRAWING.

BUT IT DOESN'T MATTER ANYMORE.

I DON'T WANT ANYTHING.
I WON'T REACH FOR ANYTHING, AND I WON'T REFUSE ANYTHING THAT COMES.

MY WISH WILL NEVER BE GRANTED ANYWAY.

IN A FICTIONAL WORLD, YOU CAN PORTRAY ANY WISH, NO MATTER HOW UNATTAINABLE IT IS IN REALITY.

HOW WORTHLESS.

交通
WORTH-LESS.
WORTH-LESS.
WORTH-LESS.
WORTHLESS, WORTHLESS, WORTHLESS.

DREAM AS MUCH AS YOU WANT— REALITY WON'T CHANGE.
FICTION CAN'T CHANGE REALITY.

HAAH...

I WISH...
..."I" HAD NEVER DRAWN THAT PICTURE.
IF NOT FOR THAT PICTURE, THERE WOULD HAVE BEEN NO RUMORS...

...AND "ART ROOM SHIJIMA-SAN" WOULD NEVER HAVE EXISTED.

IT'S TIME TO GRANT YOUR WISH!

MY WISH...?

MY WISH IS— ...

SLASH
OPERATING ROOM

POOR THING...
PSST
TOO YOUNG TO DIE.
SO YOUNG TOO...
PSST
PSST

MY WISH...
...IS TO DO WHAT I WAS BORN FOR.
HER DISEASE IS INCUR-ABLE.
SO THERE'S ONLY ONE THING I CAN DO.
BEFORE MEI SHIJIMA...
...FINISHES THAT DRAWING...
...AND ASKS TO DONATE IT...

...I WILL KILL HER...
...AND ERASE "MYSELF."

CLATTER
MEI-CHAN, WATCH OUT!!
OH!
GASP
SWOOSH
EEK!
ACK!
WOBBLE
CRAAASH
CLANK
ARE YOU OKAY!?
OOOOW...
I THINK SO...

YOU...

YOU LOOK JUST LIKE ME...
WHO ARE YOU...?
......
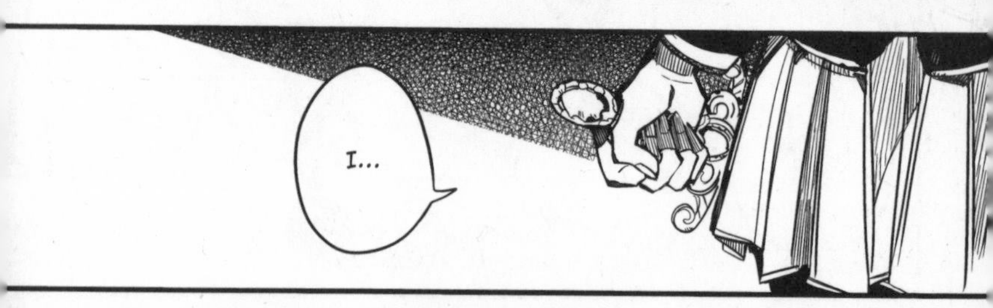
I...
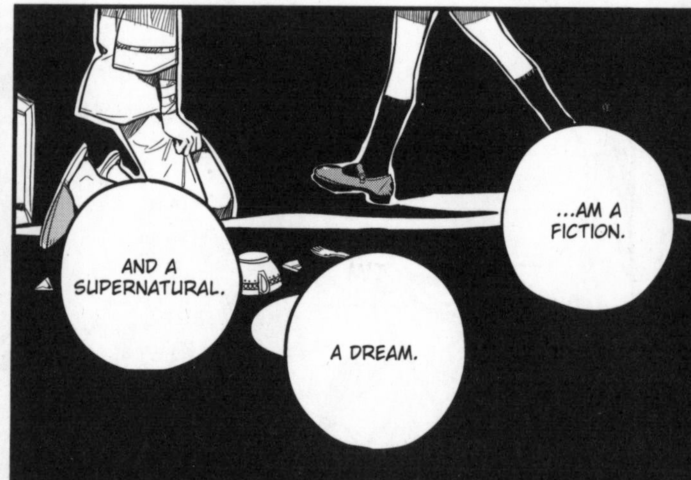
...AM A FICTION.
A DREAM.
AND A SUPERNATURAL.

SHFF

I'VE WANTED TO APOLOGIZE TO YOU FOR SO LONG.
I'M SORRY...
...MEI SHIJIMA.

I COULDN'T DO WHAT YOU ASKED ME.
I WAS BORN TO PROTECT YOU...
...BUT I COULDN'T.
SO THE THEME IS TOWERS, HUH?
HMMM... WHAT KIND OF TOWER SHOULD I DRAW?
ART PROGRAM
THIRD YEAR FINAL EXAM
ART THEME:
TOWERS
WRITTEN EXAM
...I KNOW!

むく…
RISE
THIS TOWER IS AN ATELIER.
INSIDE IT, THERE'S AN ALTERNATE ME.
SKRIT
SHE'S HAPPY, HEALTHY, AND CREATES ART.

ALL RIGHT!
LET'S GO WITH THAT!
I WANT TO AT LEAST BE HAPPY INSIDE MY PICTURES, AFTER ALL.
......
HEY...
...IS IT FUN IN YOUR WORLD?

SILLY QUESTION! THAT'S WHAT I'M ABOUT TO DRAW!
THNK
ROLL
OH.
MY BRUSH...
CREAK
TWANG
PRICK
OW!
...OH YEAH.
I'M KIND OF SICK IN THIS WORLD.
BUT I'M SURE I'LL GET BETTER.

UNTIL THEN...

...WILL YOU KEEP DRAWING PICTURES FOR ME?
IF YOU DO, I THINK THAT WILL KEEP ME GOING.
HA-HA... I'M BEING SILLY.
TALKING TO MYSELF LIKE THIS.

...ALL RIGHT.
I'LL KEEP DRAWING...
...IN YOUR PLACE.
SO DON'T WORRY.

IT'S GOING TO BE OKAY.
OKAY!
WAIT... HUH?
WHO AM I TALKING TO...?
I...

...AM THE IDEAL SELF THAT YOU WISHED FOR.
I AM ONE OF YOUR DRAWINGS.
YOU CREATED ME SO THAT YOU COULD LIVE.
BUT FICTION CAN'T CHANGE REALITY.
I COULDN'T SAVE YOU.
FAR FROM IT.

I BECAME THE SOURCE OF TWISTED RUMORS.
I HEARD SHE KILLED HERSELF—

I CAN'T LET THAT HAPPEN.
AND I WON'T.
MY WISH...
...WAS TO DO WHAT YOU CREATED ME TO DO—TO PROTECT YOU.

GRIP

MEI-CHAN!
WHAM
KACRASH
URK!
BUT IF I CAN'T SAVE YOU...
...AT LEAST...

...I CAN STOP THOSE RUMORS.
I'LL KEEP MYSELF, THIS WORTHLESS FICTION, FROM HURTING YOU.
I WILL...
...PROTECT YOUR TRUTH.

YOU...
SPOOK 55
PERFECT NONSENSE

...ARE MY DRAWING ...?

AM I...

...AM I GOING TO DIE?
...
I KNOW YOUR PAIN.

YOUR ANXIETY.
YOUR FEAR.
I WAS THERE...
...THROUGH ALL THOSE SLEEPLESS NIGHTS.

THROUGH IT ALL, YOU KEPT SMILING, BELIEVING IN YOUR FUTURE.
BUT THE FUTURE YOU WISHED FOR WILL NEVER COME.

YOU ARE GOING TO DIE.
CLAMP
STOP IT!!
STOP.. STOP THIS.
HOW CAN YOU SAY THOSE TERRIBLE THINGS TO HER...!?

WHAM
EEK!

I DON'T NEED YOU TO UNDERSTAND.

I DOUBT ANYTHING I SAY...
...WILL BE ENOUGH TO CONVINCE YOU.

SUPERNATURALS AND THE LIVING CAN NEVER UNDERSTAND ONE ANOTHER.
I...
Iooo
...HAVE TO SAVE HER.

I AM GOING TO SAVE YOU, YASHIRO.

OH...

N...
NO ...!!
THOONK

HUSH
WOW, THAT WAS A CLOSE ONE.
MEI-CHAN!!
WHEW!
TCH!

JUST LET ME...

ぱしっ
GRAB

ガッ
FLING
HI-YAH!
ばっ
ぐるん
WHIRL

ドッ
THUD

WHAM

YOU KNOW...
...I'M GETTING THE FEELING...

BOOP
つん

...THAT YOU...
...REALLY, REALLY LIKE ME!

...HUH?

ビビ
ビシ
BZT
BZT
!
ピシ
ッ
CRACK

WH-
WHAT
...!?
ぐらぐら
SHAKE
SHAKE
SHAKE
HEY!
ピョン!
POING
NENE-CHAN, LET'S GO!
ぱし
SNATCH

たたた
TEP TEP TEP
MEI-CHAAAN...
I THOUGHT SHE WAS GOING TO KILL YOU...!
NOW, NOW, DON'T CRY.
WHY...!?

WHY ARE YOU RUNNING FROM ME!?
I EXIST FOR YOU!
WHY ARE YOU REJECTING ME!?

I...

KRIK

CRUMB
CLATTER
CLATTER

THE HOSPITAL'S FALLING APART...!
MEI-CHAN, WHERE ARE WE GOING?
SHAKE
SHAKE
SHAKE

WE'RE GOING TO THIS WORLD'S EXIT.
THE EXIT ...!?
SO YOU REALLY DID KNOW HOW TO GET OUT...

YOU SEE...
...THIS WORLD IS MY DREAM.
YOUR DREAM?
SO ALL I HAVE TO DO IS OPEN MY EYES...
...AND YOU SHOULD GO BACK WHERE YOU BELONG, NENE-CHAN.

WHAT DO WE ...?
LEAVE IT TO ME!
REALITY'S SO INCONVENIENT IN LOTSA WAYS.
BUT IN THIS WORLD, I CAN DO ANYTHING.

OOPS.

THE FLOOR...
CRUMBLE
ガラ
CRUMBLE
ガラ
CRUMBLE
ガラ

LIKE THIS...
CLAMP
BOING
SEE! ♥
SKFF

BUT.

...LOOKS LIKE I DREAMED TOO LONG TODAY.
IT'S ABOUT TIME I WAKE UP.

THIS IS THE WAY OUT...?
YUP.
AT THE TOP OF THOSE STAIRS.

LET'S GO.

I CAN SEE THROUGH THEM...
ドキドキ
BADUM BADUM
そろ〜
SLOOOW

ズリッ
ZUM

WH-WH-WHY!? I CAN'T CLIMB THE STA—
!?
WHOA THERE.
ブル
TREMBLE
AH!
ブル
TREMBLE
IS IT BECAUSE MY F-F-F-F-F-F-F-F-FEET ARE SO FAT!?
スゥ…
SWOOO
ブル
TREMBLE

......

...THESE STAIRS LEAD TO MY REALITY.

I BET YOU HAVE TO GET BACK TO A DIFFERENT PLACE, NENE-CHAN.

WELL... I GUESS THIS IS GOOD-BYE, THEN...
...NENE-CHAN.

THESE STAIRS LEAD TO MEI-CHAN'S REALITY...

BUT WHEN SHE GETS BACK...
...WILL SHE DIE?

......
?

SQUEEZE
ぎゅ...
ARE...
ARE YOU REALLY GOING UP THERE?
I MEAN, MEI-CHAN...

...AREN'T YOU SCARED?
...

ぽん
PAT

HEH...
I WONDER ...
...WHERE YOU CAME FROM, NENE-CHAN.

MAYBE YOU'RE FROM THE FUTURE?
!
HEE HEE.
AM I RIGHT?
IN THAT CASE...
す
SLIP
WAIT!!

D—
DON'T GO...
PLEASE DON'T GO!

I DON'T WANT TO BE A MEANINGLESS FICTION THAT DOES NOTHING BUT HURT YOU.
I CAN'T DO IT... I JUST CAN'T.

YOU AREN'T MEANING-LESS.

REALITY CAN REALLY HURT SOMETIMES...

SO WE CLOSE OUR EYES AND DREAM...
...TO SEE US THROUGH TO ANOTHER TOMORROW.

YOU ARE MY DRAWING.
MY DREAM.

AND MY HOPE.

IT'S BECAUSE YOU'RE HERE THAT I WILL OPEN MY EYES AGAIN TODAY.

IT'S BECAUSE OF YOU THAT I CAN GO ON LIVING.

AND HEY.

WHAT'S WRONG WITH BEING A SUPER-NATURAL!?
ばしばしばし
BASH BASH BASH
YOU'RE GOING DOWN IN HISTORY AS A SCHOOL GHOST STORY!

ビッ!
FWIP
THAT'S SO COOL!

こつん
KONK

...THANKS FOR COMING TO SEE ME...
...MY OTHER SELF.

AS SHE
DISAP-
PEARED
INTO THE
DISTANCE...

...SHIJIMA-SAN...
...WATCHED HER GO WITHOUT SAYING A WORD.
...ADI...
...DISH...

WAKE UP, RADISH!

...?
???
...??
??
OH!
YOU'RE AWAKE.

HEY, RADISH-SENPAI'S AWAKE!
STOP CALLING HER THAT!
TEP TEP TEP

MITSUBA-KUN...
KOU-KUN!

BEEEEAM
ぱあああ
GOOD MORNING, SENPAI!

ARE YOU OKAY!?
YOU'RE NOT HURT, ARE YOU!?
WAAAH!
I'M JUST FINE!
ANYWAY, HOW DID YOU GET HERE?

WELL, IT'S A LONG STORY, BUT...

FIRST, I'D LIKE YOU TO TAKE A LOOK AT THIS!
TWIRL
くるっ

BAM
WE APPREHENDED No. 4!!
HEH HEH!!
WAAAAH! SHIJIMA-SAAAAN!!?
THIS HAPPENED THE SECOND I GOT BACK...
HAAAH...
I HATE PEOPLE WHO IMMEDIATELY RESORT TO VIOLENCE.
HUP!
...WELL?
SWOOSH
CLAAANG
WHAT...
RE YOU
ING TO
NOW...

...SOON-TO-BE-DEAD YASHIRO-SAN?

!
SHE SAID IT...
!!?

I...

I...

...DON'T KNOW WHAT TO DO.
I CAN'T BE LIKE MEI-CHAN.
I'M NOT READY TO MAKE UP MY MIND, BUT...

...I'M GOING TO SEE HANAKO-KUN!

BECAUSE...

...I HAVE SOMETHING I WANT TO SAY TO HIM!
TO BE CONTINUED IN TOILET-BOUND HANAKO-KUN 12!

TRANSLATION NOTES

Common Honorifics
no honorific: Indicates familiarity or closeness; if used without permission or reason, addressing someone in this manner would constitute an insult.
-san: The Japanese equivalent of Mr./Mrs./Miss. If a situation calls for politeness, this is the fail-safe honorific.
-sama: Conveys great respect; may also indicate that the social status of the speaker is lower than that of the addressee.
-kun: Used most often when referring to boys, this indicates affection or familiarity. Occasionally used by older men among their peers, but it may also be used by anyone referring to a person of lower standing.
-chan: An affectionate honorific indicating familiarity used mostly in reference to girls; also used in reference to cute persons or animals of either gender.
-senpai: A suffix used to address upperclassmen or more experienced coworkers.
-sensei: A respectful term for teachers, artists, or high-level professionals.

Page 2
In the original Japanese, the chapter titles in this volume are all five-syllable words ending in *goto*, which is written with either the kanji for "word" or "thing." This translation reflects that parallelism with the recurring "perfect" and "painting" motifs in each of its chapter titles, as the title used for the previous volume's chapters, "Picture Perfect," was also originally a five-syllable word ending in *goto* (*esoragoto*, meaning "fabrication").

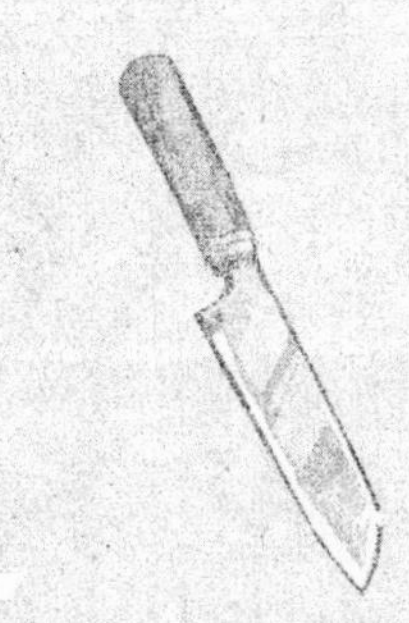

Page 80
Previously, Shijima's name has always been written in *katakana*, a syllabary used to phonetically spell words out. However, the living Shijima uses kanji to spell her name, which confirms that the first kanji in Shijima means "four." Very fitting that she became School Mystery No. 4, just like how Mitsuba, whose name's first kanji means "three," became School Mystery No. 3.

Page 177
The honorific *-tan* is a cutesy way to refer to women one is close to; it's even less formal than *-chan*.

TEACH ME, SHIJIMA-SAN
— THE BOSS —

CUT SCENE FROM CHAPTER 55

SPECIAL THANKS

EKE-CHAN OMAYU-TAN YUUJI-CHAN
RUI-CHAN REYU-CHAN ANNE-CHAN KURUMI-CHAN

MY EDITOR, IMANITY
COVER DESIGN, NAKAMURA-SAMA

AND YOU

DO ON HIS TIME OFF?

ON SALE NOW!

WHAT DOES HANAKO-KUN

After-School Hanako-Kun

AidaIro

Translation: Alethea Nibley and Athena Nibley
Lettering: Kimberly Pham

Yen Press
150 West 30th Street, 19th Floor
New York, NY 10001

Visit us at yenpress.com • facebook.com/yenpress • twitter.com/yenpress • yenpress.tumblr.com • instagram.com/yenpress

First Yen Press Print Edition: September 2021
Originally published as an ebook in May 2020 by Yen Press.

Yen Press is an imprint of Yen Press, LLC.
The Yen Press name and logo are trademarks of Yen Press, LLC.

The publisher is not responsible for websites (or their content) that are not owned by the publisher.

Library of Congress Control Number: 2019953610

ISBN: 978-1-9753-1681-5 (paperback)

10 9 8 7 6 5 4 3 2 1

TPA

Printed in South Korea

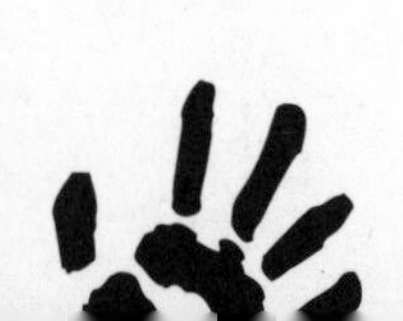